Dedicated to the spirit of Florida State,
which passes on the traditions contained
in this book since 1851.

www.mascotbooks.com

Campus Explorers: The Search for Osceola and Renegade

For more information, please contact:
Mascot Books
620 Herndon Parkway, Suite 320
Herndon, VA 20170
info@mascotbooks.com

CPSIA Code: PRT0618A
ISBN-13: 978-1-68401-202-2

Printed in the United States

CAMPUS EXPLORERS
The Search for Osceola and Renegade

Stuart Santos & Jon Smith

Illustrated by Yoko Matsuoka

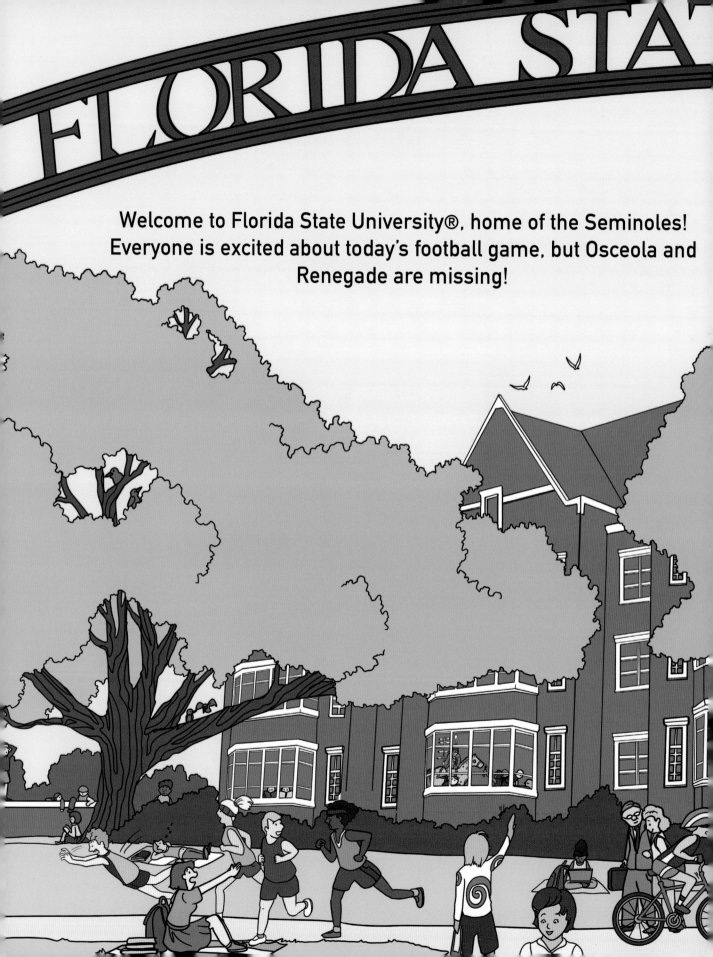

Welcome to Florida State University®, home of the Seminoles! Everyone is excited about today's football game, but Osceola and Renegade are missing!

The game can't start until they arrive at the stadium!
We need your help to find them again
so they can lead the Noles on to another win!

Westcott Fountain is the first place to look. It's a popular landmark for birthday traditions and graduation photos.

Could they have gone for a swim in the fountain or
taken a nap on a bench?
Look high and low for where they might be.
Check the steps of the building or the shade of a tree!

Next, let's search Landis Green and the Legacy Fountain—a beautiful lawn where students can relax and play.

Make sure to stop at Strozier Library on your journey, where students read and learn.

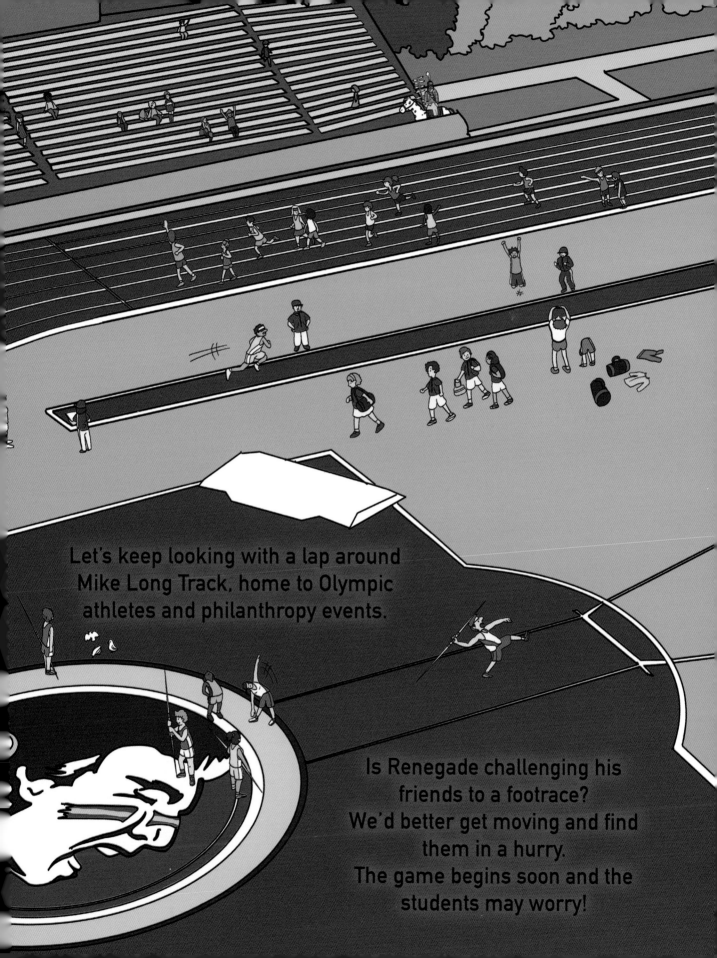

Let's keep looking with a lap around Mike Long Track, home to Olympic athletes and philanthropy events.

Is Renegade challenging his friends to a footrace? We'd better get moving and find them in a hurry. The game begins soon and the students may worry!

Next, we should visit the Flying High Circus.
This student-led performance is one of a kind. Could they be dangling from above on the flying trapeze?!

Inside the big tent, performers soar through the air,
but kickoff is soon and we need our school spirit there!

One of our last stops is the Unconquered Statue.
Students and alumni gather here wearing the garnet and gold!
Will we be able to locate them with all these people about?

Fans are in a frenzy—Osceola and Renegade have still not been found!
Look closely through the crowd. They're sure to be around!

We've finally arrived inside Doak Campbell Stadium!™ The players are warming up and the fans are filing in.

Look closely! There! In the center of the field! Osceola and Renegade made it in time!

Now that they are together and the fans are in their seats, we can snatch victory from the jaws of defeat!

Congratulations! You did it! The Seminoles remain unconquered!

We couldn't have found them without your help!

The game can now start with the planting of the spear,

and with it begins another championship year!

Have a book idea?
Contact us at:

info@mascotbooks.com | www.mascotbooks.com